THE VERY HUNGRY CATERPILLAR

by Eric Carle

Hamish Hamilton • London

THE BAD-TEMPERED LADYBIRD
BROWN BEAR, BROWN BEAR, WHAT DO YOU SEE?
DO YOU WANT TO BE MY FRIEND?
DRAW ME A STAR
DREAM SNOW
FROM HEAD TO TOE
A HOUSE FOR HERMIT CRAB
LITTLE CLOUD
THE MIXED-UP CHAMELEON
1, 2, 3 TO THE ZOO
POLAR BEAR, POLAR BEAR, WHAT DO YOU HEAR?
ROOSTER'S OFF TO SEE THE WORLD
THE TINY SEED
TODAY IS MONDAY
THE VERY BUSY SPIDER
THE VERY QUIET CRICKET

HAMISH HAMILTON LTD

Published by the Penguin Group
Penguin Books Ltd, 27 Wrights Lane, London W8 5TZ, England
Penguin Books USA Inc., 375 Hudson Street, New York, New York 10014, USA
Penguin Books Australia Ltd, Ringwood, Victoria, Australia
Penguin Books Canada Ltd, 10 Alcorn Avenue, Toronto, Ontario, Canada M4V 3B2
Penguin Books (NZ) Ltd, Private Bag 102902, NSMC, Auckland, New Zealand

On the World Wide Web at: www.penguin.com

Penguin Books Ltd, Registered Offices: Harmondsworth, Middlesex, England

First published in the USA by The World Publishing Company, Cleveland and New York
Published in Great Britain by Hamish Hamilton Ltd 1970
This edition published 2000
10 9 8 7 6 5 4 3 2 1

Copyright © Eric Carle, 1969

All rights reserved.
Without limiting the rights under copyright reserved above, no part of this publication may
be reproduced, stored in or introduced into a retrieval system, or transmitted, in any form or by
any means (electronic, mechanical, photocopying, recording or otherwise), without the prior
written permission of both the copyright owner and the above publisher of this book

Printed in China by Imago Publishing Limited

British Library Cataloguing in Publication Data
A CIP catalogue record for this book is available from the British Library

ISBN 0–241–14106–0

For my sister Christa

In the light of the moon
a little egg lay on a leaf.

BELFAST PUBLIC LIBRARIES

One Sunday morning the warm sun came up and – pop! – out of the egg came a tiny and very hungry caterpillar.

He started to look for some food.

On Thursday
he ate through
four strawberries,
but he was still
hungry.

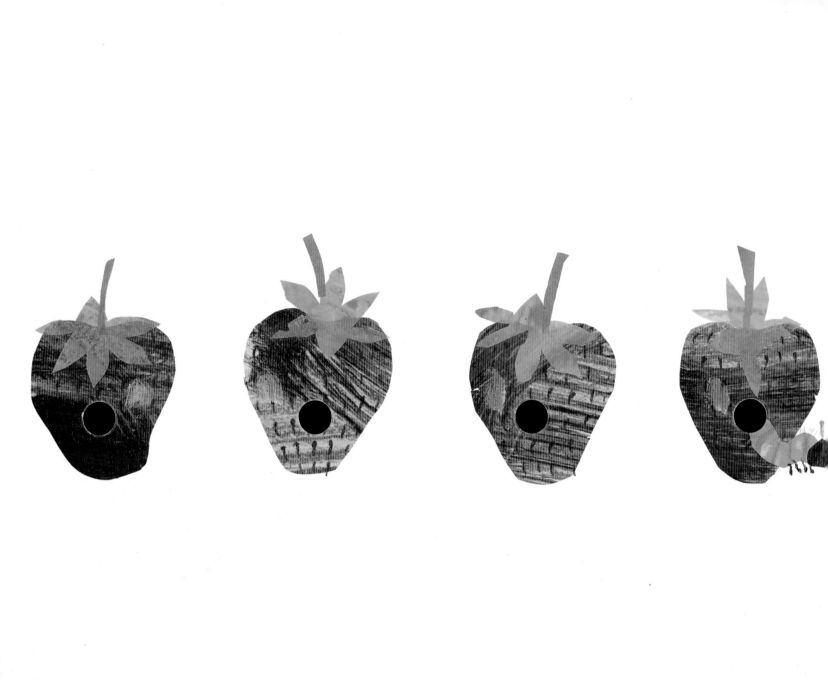

On Friday
he ate through
five oranges,
but he was still
hungry.

On Saturday
he ate through
one piece of
chocolate cake, one ice-cream cone, one pickle, one slice of Swiss cheese, one slice of salami,

one lollipop, one piece of cherry pie, one sausage, one cupcake, and one slice of watermelon.

That night he had a stomachache!

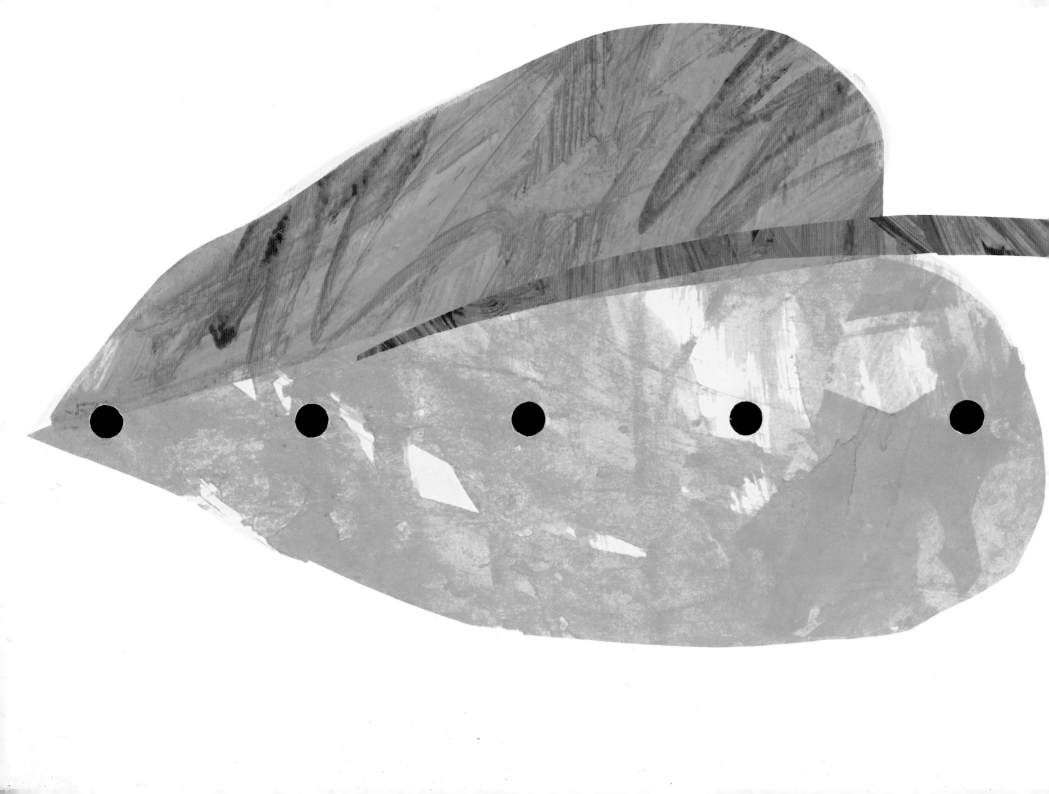

The next day was Sunday again.
The caterpillar ate through
one nice green leaf,
and after that he felt
much better.

Now he wasn't hungry any more – and he wasn't a little caterpillar any more.
He was a big, fat caterpillar.

He built a small house, called a cocoon, around himself. He stayed inside for more than two weeks. Then he nibbled a hole in the cocoon, pushed his way out and …

he was a beautiful butterfly!

BELFAST PUBLIC LIBRARIES